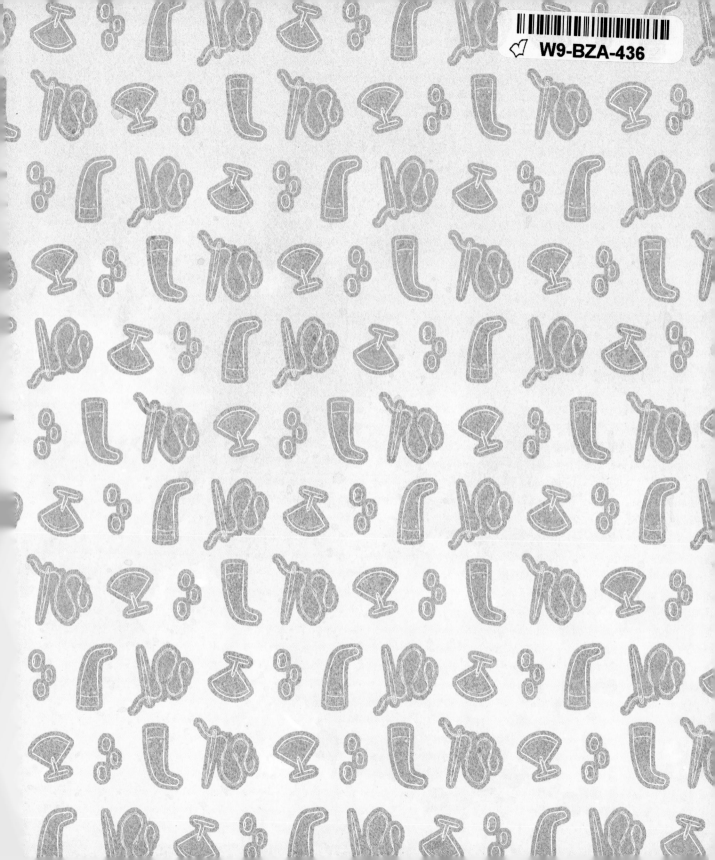

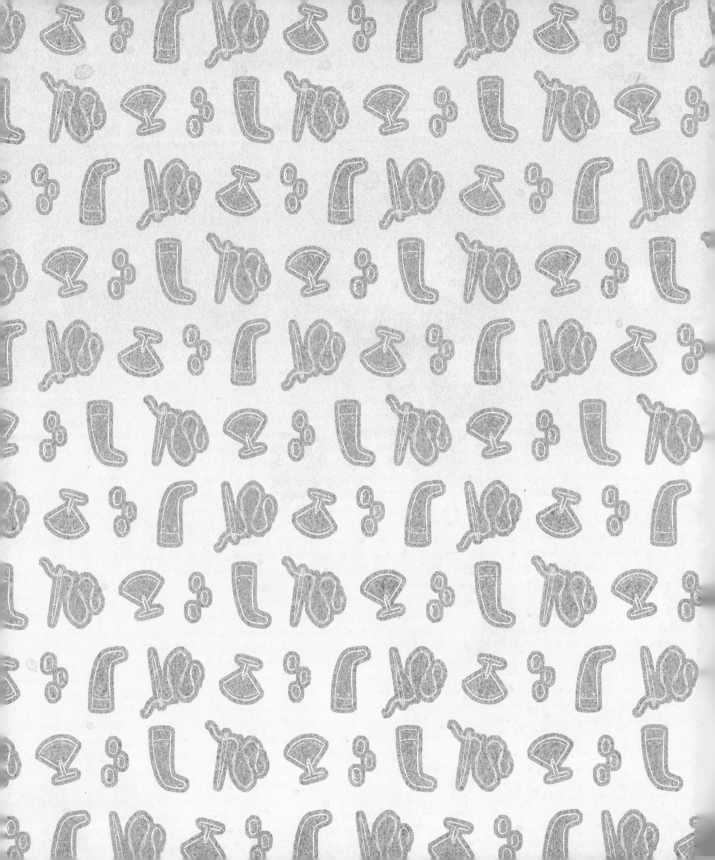

UNA HUNA?

Ukpik Learns to Sew

PUBLISHED BY INHABIT MEDIA INC.
www.inhabitmedia.com

Inhabit Media Inc. (Iqaluit) P.O. Box 11125, Iqaluit, Nunavut, X0A 1H0

Editors: Neil Christopher and Kelly Ward
Art directors: Danny Christopher and Astrid Arijanto

This project was made possible in part by the Government of Canada.

We acknowledge the support of the Canada Council for the Arts for our publishing program.

Printed in Canada

ISBN: 978-177227-433-2

Library and Archives Canada Cataloguing in Publication

Title: Una huna? : Ukpik learns to sew / by Susan Aglukark ; illustrated by Amiel Sandland and Rebecca Brook.
Other titles: Ukpik learns to sew
Names: Aglukark, Susan, 1967- author. | Sandland, Amiel, illustrator. | Brook, Rebecca, illustrator.
Identifiers: Canadiana 20220160066 | ISBN 9781772274332 (hardcover)
Subjects: LCGFT: Picture books.
Classification: LCC PS8601G58 U53 2022 | DDC jC813/.6—dc23

Una Huna?

Ukpik Learns to Sew

by Susan Aglukark

illustrated by

Amiel Sandland and Rebecca Brook

It was early fall in Ukpik's camp, and she was playing with her puppy, Uummat, between two tents. Uummat suddenly began to bark toward the open tundra. In the distance, Ukpik saw three small figures walking toward the camp. She immediately recognized them as her father, her uncle, and her cousin Anguti. The men had gone out hunting that afternoon after the Captain and his ship had departed. The Captain visited their camp once a year to trade with Ukpik's *ataata*, her *father*.

"*Anaana*, I see Ataata, *Akkak*, and Anguti!" Ukpik called to her mother. "I am going to run out to meet them."

"Yes, but be watchful," Anaana replied.

Ukpik ran out onto the tundra toward the men, with Uummat at her heels. As she got closer, Anguti ran to meet her.

"Did you catch anything?" Ukpik asked.

"Yes!" Anguti replied excitedly. "We caught five caribou. Ataata and Akkak have most of them, and the skins."

"Oh, Anaana will be happy," Ukpik replied. "She has been talking about trying something special with her new *sungaujait*, the *beads* Ataata traded the Captain for. I'm not sure what those are, but she won't let me play with them, so they must be important."

Anguti shrugged. "*Aamai*," he said, indicating that he didn't know.

As the group got closer to the camp, with Ukpik and Anguti leading the way, Ukpik's anaana stood by the tent, happy to see them return. When Ataata reached her, she looked quickly through the furs and smiled, knowing she would have enough caribou furs with which to start her project. She had something very special in mind to make with her new beads, and she needed several skins to make it.

"*Naammaktuujaaliqtut amiit. Looks like you got enough furs. Quvianaq! I am happy!*" Anaana said with a smile.

Ukpik walked over to her mother and asked excitedly, "What are you going to make, Anaana? Can you tell me?"

Anaana looked at Ukpik and said with a giggle, "You will see, Ukpik. You must be patient. You will like it. I may even need your help with this project."

Ukpik walked away, very happy about the idea of helping her mother on a project with the colourful little beads.

The next morning, Anaana began to clean the caribou skins. Ukpik knelt right beside her anaana, watching and waiting.

"Ukpik, go and get the little *ulu* that your *ataatatsiaq*, your *grandfather*, made for you," Anaana said. "I will need your help cleaning the caribou skins, but you must listen to me and be very careful with your ulu."

"Yes, Anaana!" Ukpik called. She ran into the *tupiq*, the *tent*, to fetch the ulu her grandfather had made for her, which she had stored in a safe place.

When she returned, Ukpik couldn't help but ask, "So Anaana, will I get to work with the beads, too?"

"Yes, Ukpik," Anaana replied. "But first I will need your help with the skins. We must prepare those, and then we will get to the beads."

With her ulu in her hand, Ukpik sat down next to her mother. Anaana placed a part of the caribou skin on Ukpik's lap.

"Take your ulu and feel along the skin. You will feel little pieces of rough skin; these pieces are extra bits of fat that did not get removed in the skinning of the caribou. They need to be removed so that this fur will dry as smooth as possible. This will make the finished garment much cleaner looking. Cut off these little pieces of fat right at the end," Anaana said.

Anaana took Ukpik's hand and guided it along the skin gently. Ukpik felt a slight change in texture and excitedly asked, "You mean like this?"

"Yes," Anaana replied, "just like that. Be very careful not to cut yourself."

Ukpik and Anaana spent the rest of the day cleaning the caribou skins.

On the other side of the tent, Ataata, Akkak, and Anguti were sharpening pieces of twigs that would be used to stretch the cleaned caribou skins. The skins would be stretched out as tightly as possible across the land and would stay pinned to the earth for many days until they were dry.

For the next few days, Ukpik ran out to check on the skins regularly to see if they were dry enough for the next step of the process.

On the third day, Ukpik asked, "Anaana, how much longer do the skins have to sit there?"

"Not much longer, Ukpik," Anaana said. "We have to be sure they are properly dried because we cannot waste any of these skins. Remember, I said you would have to be patient."

"Okay, Anaana, but when do we start working with the sungaujait? Is there anything I can do with them while we wait?" Ukpik couldn't hide her impatience at getting her hands on the beautiful beads.

Anaana thought for a moment and decided to string a row of beads that Ukpik could follow. If Ukpik could follow Anaana's pattern, the beads could become part of the finished project.

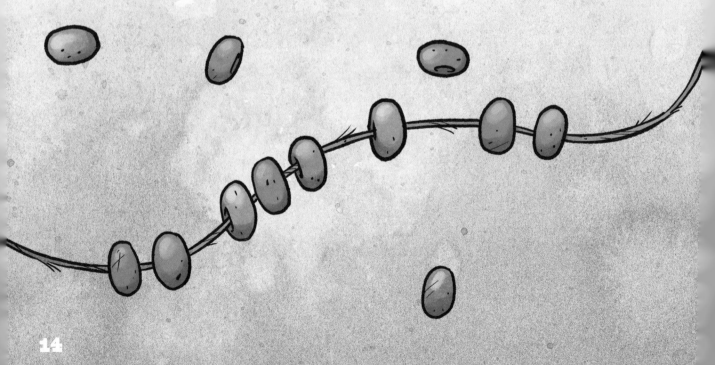

"Follow this beading pattern," Anaana said, handing Ukpik the first strand of beads. "Show me a string of these beads when you are done. If it works well, then you can make me ten strings."

Ukpik eagerly grabbed the beads and began working on the pattern. She was determined to get it exactly right.

By the fifth day, the skins were perfectly dry, and
Anaana and Ukpik, with Ataata's help, gathered the
skins and piled them up.

"What do we do next, Anaana?" Ukpik asked.

"Well, now we have to soften the skins," Anaana replied.

Anaana took one of the skins, bunched it up beneath her
feet, and began to gently step on it. Ukpik watched her closely.

"We need to crunch the skins beneath our feet until they
are as soft as possible," Anaana said. "Here, come stand with
me."

Anaana took Ukpik's hand
and, facing each other, they
begin crunching the skins
beneath their feet.

Ukpik giggled.
"This is fun, Anaana!"

A few days later, Ataata gifted Ukpik a small *sakuut, a tool for softening skins,* that he had fashioned himself from caribou bone.

"This is a sakuut," Ataata told her. "Your mother will show you how to use this properly, but it will help to soften the caribou skin."

Ataata hugged Ukpik and left Ukpik and her mother to their work. Anaana showed Ukpik how to use the sakuut by practising on a small piece of skin.

"Start very gently. Don't force it," Anaana said. "Get used to how the end of the sakuut slides along the skin." Anaana gently directed Ukpik's hands over the caribou hide while Ukpik held the hide in place with her knee.

Ukpik watched her mother working with her sakuut. She mimicked her movements, and Anaana peeked at Ukpik from time to time with a smile on her face.

"Anaana, does softening the skin make it easier to sew?" Ukpik asked.

"Yes, Ukpik, it does," Anaana replied. "It also makes it easier to make tighter stitches, and to be more accurate with our work. You must always remember, Ukpik, that we have only what we have. These five furs are all that we can use for this project, and for a few other winter pieces. We cannot waste any of it."

For the rest of the afternoon, Ukpik and Anaana sat outside softening the skins.

A few more days passed, and the hides that had been softened were finally ready to have the pattern cut out.

Anaana cut the pattern and settled herself to begin sewing. Ukpik was getting set to play with her friends when she heard her mother call her, "Ukpik, *qairaallagit*; Ukpik, *come here, please*!"

Ukpik ran back to where her mother was seated just outside the tent. Anaana patted the spot beside her and said to Ukpik, "You will sit with me and try out some sewing before you can go play with your friends."

Ukpik's friend Qopak walked over and asked, "Can I sew something, too?"

"Of course, Qopak," Anaana replied. "Sit beside me here." Anaana knew to keep Ukpik and Qopak separated, or the sewing lesson would quickly become a giggling match.

Anaana had prepared small *pualuuk* patterns, *mitten* patterns, from leftover fur.

"Are mittens our big project, Anaana?" Ukpik asked, a bit disappointed.

Anaana smiled. "The mittens are for practise," she replied.

Anaana handed Ukpik and Qopak each a needle, a string of sinew, and the first two parts of the mitten patterns. The girls began sewing.

After sewing their mittens for a while, both Ukpik and Qopak were very restless and ready to move on from sewing to exploring the tundra.

"Anaana, how much more do I need to do?" Ukpik asked, setting her work in her lap.

"Well, how warm do you want your hands to be this winter?" Anaana replied. "Ukpik, everything we do is in preparation for the next thing. You must learn to sew in order to be prepared for the next season and the season after that. Everything you sew must fit you as well as possible, otherwise it will not serve you well for its season. You have grown this year, and so we need to replace your mittens. These should be good for the next couple of winters, but then you will need to make another pair, and possibly you will have to learn to make your own *kamiik*, your *sealskin boots*, as well.

"You must begin your lessons now so you know how to do the right stitches for each pattern. The size and shape of the stitches matter, Ukpik, and to get these right, you must practise. You and Qopak will practise every morning from today until your mittens are done."

Ukpik understood and sensed that what her mother was telling her was very important. She focused her attention on her sewing. After a bit more time had passed, Ukpik stopped to take a look at her stitches. They were loose and crooked. Then she peeked at her mother's work. Her stitches were perfect.

"Anaana, I will never be able to do this!" Ukpik exclaimed in frustration.

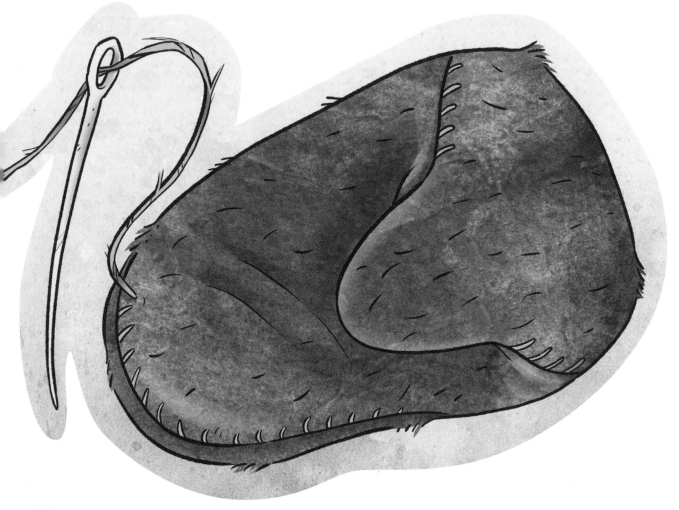

"You will not get it perfect in a day, Ukpik. That is why I say you and Qopak will join me here every morning and practise your stitching before you go out and play," Anaana said with a smile. "Don't fret, love, you will get it. It just takes time and practise."

Ukpik took one more look at her project, then handed it over to Anaana. Anaana hugged Ukpik and sent her off to play with Qopak and Anguti.

The three friends settled on a little hill overlooking the water and watched the mast of a ship in the distance. Ukpik was reminded of the beautiful sungaujait, and how she still wished Anaana would let her sew with them.

"Ukpik, what was your anaana teaching you?" Anguti asked.

Ukpik looked down at her hands. "Anaana says that my hands have grown out of my mittens, and that I have to learn to make myself new ones," Ukpik replied thoughtfully. "I did not realize how much work it is to keep us all clothed and warm, Anguti. It is a lot of work, but I am enjoying learning."

Anguti and Qopak both looked down at their hands, and then at each other.

"I guess ours have grown too . . ." Anguti said. "What does that mean, Ukpik? Do I have to make my own mittens, too?" Ukpik and Qopak looked at Anguti for a moment. He had a look of fear on his face that made the girls begin to laugh.

"No, silly," Qopak said. "You don't have to learn how to sew. Unless you want to."

"Ahh, no thanks," Anguti replied. "I am happy with what I am learning as a hunter."

They all laughed and looked out toward the mast, which was slowly disappearing into the horizon.

While the children played, Anaana quietly snuck out her beading project and carried on with it privately. She was keeping this piece secret from Ukpik, waiting for the right time to show her what she was making for her. Anaana and Ataata kept an eye and an ear out for Ukpik while she worked, so that Ukpik would not see the surprise Anaana had in store.

"That is a lovely *tuilik* you are making for Ukpik," Ataata said, smiling at Anaana as she worked on the *parka*.

"Yes, I am enjoying the challenge," Anaana replied. "I am realizing how much my mother and grandmother had to learn—having to teach themselves about patterns and preparing furs. I have learned what they taught me, and now I must teach Ukpik. She has a lot to learn, but I want her to enjoy her lessons, too. Things changed with the Captain's arrival. Now Ukpik and the other children know that there is another world out there. They are growing up with this knowledge—what they can imagine has changed, which means they have changed."

"Yes, it does feel like each new thing we learn is changing us," Ataata agreed. "We have a beautiful past and traditional ways. It is sometimes hard to see how much will be kept alive through them," Ataata said, gesturing toward the children playing on the shore.

"Our ancestors were very clever people," Anaana said with a smile. "I wish for my Ukpik to know that her world is a beautiful one, and that all the things she is learning come from beautiful ancestors."

Anaana and Ataata looked out toward the ship's mast as it slowly glided away from the camp. At the water's edge, they could see Ukpik, Anguti, and Qopak happily playing with Uummat, throwing stones out into the lake.

GLOSSARY OF INUKTUT WORDS

Inuktut is the word for Inuit languages spoken in Canada, including Inuktitut and Inuinnaqtun. The pronunciation guides in this book are intended to support non-Inuktut speakers in their reading of Inuktut words. These pronunciations are not exact representations of how the words are pronounced by Inuktut speakers.

For more resources on how to pronounce Inuktut words, visit inhabitmedia.com/inuitnipingit.

Term	Pronunciation	Meaning
Aamai.	AH-mah-ee	I don't know.
Akkak	AH-kahk	Uncle
Anaana	ah-NAH-nah	Mother
Anguti	AH-ngoo-tee	name, meaning "man"
Ataata	ah-TAH-tah	Father
Ataatatsiaq	ah-TAH-taht-see-ahk	Grandfather
kamiik	kah-MEEK	a pair of skin boots

Naammaktuujaaliqtut amiit.	NAHM-mahk-TOO-yah-leek-toot ah-MEET	Looks like you got enough furs.
pualuuk	poo-ah-LOOK	a pair of mittens
Qairaallagit.	kah-ee-RAHL-lah-gheet	Come here, please.
Qopak	KO-pahk	name
Quvianaq!	koo-VEE-ah-nahk	I am happy!
sakuut	sah-KOOT	tool for softening skins
sungaujait	soo-NGA-uu-ya-eet	beads
tuilik	to-EE-leek	woman's parka with large shoulders
tupiq	TOO-pik	tent
Ukpik	OOK-pik	name, meaning "snowy owl"
ulu	OO-loo	woman's knife
Una huna?	OO-nah HOO-nah	What is this?
Uummat	OM-maht	name, meaning "heart"

SUSAN AGLUKARK is Canada's first Inuk artist to win a Juno. She has also won a Governor General's Performing Arts Award for lifetime artistic achievement, and she is an officer of the Order of Canada. Susan holds several honorary doctorate degrees and has held command performances. During a career that has spanned more than twenty-five years, Susan's journey as a singer-songwriter has led her to reflect on who she is, where she comes from, and the importance of discovery—discovery of history, culture, and self. This time of reflection, writing, and songwriting has Susan coming back to one area of profound knowing: Inuit are an extraordinary people, deeply grounded in a culture forged by their ancestors. Her children's book, *Una Huna? What Is This?*, and her upcoming album are inspired by these reflections and cultural connections. Visit susanaglukark.com for more information.

AMIEL SANDLAND is an illustrator living in the Toronto area. He studied illustration at Seneca College, eventually specializing in comic arts and character design. He has also dabbled in layout, comics, and props making. Rarely found without a pen in hand, he enjoys drawing animals, monsters, and plants.

REBECCA BROOK is an artist working in the animation industry. While primarily a digital artist, she also works in traditional mediums such as oil paints and charcoal. Currently, she lives in Toronto but often visits her hometown of Belleville to see her family and go on adventures with her niece and nephews.

INHABIT
MEDIA

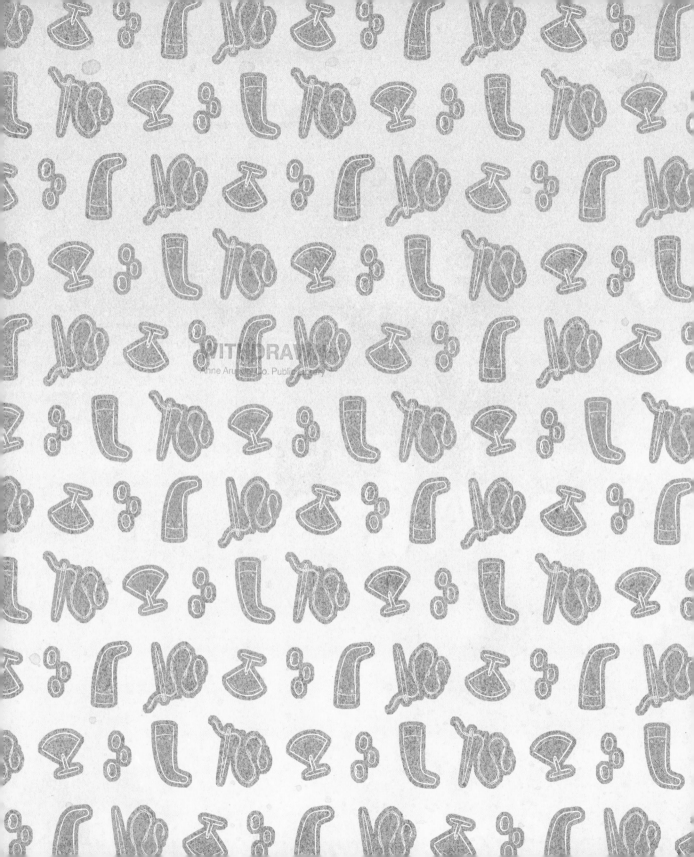